BORDERS IN THE SAND

A Novel

Andrew Calderone

AOS Publishing 2021

Copyright © 2022 Andrew Calderone

All rights reserved under International
and Pan-American copyright conventions.

ISBN: 978-1-990496-01-1

Cover Design: Lara Chauvin

Visit AOS Publishing's website:
www.aospublishing.com

For Cass

"That was the best time. The last day, the day of leaving. It was a good journey. It became different at the other end."

— V.S. Naipaul, *A Bend in the River*

GENERAL LAMENT
FEBRUARY 2174

I walked on water before I marched through hell.

Sea walls came crashing down as the ocean raced toward the island shore. Each falling wave revealed the silhouette of more ships emerging from the setting sun. I had never seen the pleasure cruises travel in such fleets before. They rarely ventured close enough to be visible. The surf at hand quickly pulled my attention from the distant vessels as the sea breeze made my eyes moist and my vision blurred. With my board underarm, I charged the white water. The lineup was full of familiar village faces. Words were few while awaiting the next set. I watched my striking husband from the surface of the water as the sea rose and fell. His skin was bathed in honey-coloured sunlight as he built sandcastles with our naked child on the beach. The sight of his swimmer's body and easy-going way with our daughter made me think of all the things I wanted to do to him once I returned to land. Explicit scenarios played out in my mind, and I felt the tide pulling me back toward the horizon. The ocean's dense, kinetic energy began its cycle. My head whipped round to witness the coming wave. I paddled. I paddled hard. It was too late. The sea took me three metres high and tossed me from my place on the crest to the flat water below. Being caught in the churning barrel beneath was a humbling thrill. I yielded to its awesome power. Saltwater infiltrated my sight, taste, and smell. I surfaced and gasped for air, quickly returning to the depths to avoid having another liquid giant bear down upon my head. Far greater forces than I pushed and pulled my tiny body below. A brief break before Poseidon's reinforcements arrived was all I needed to tug at the leather leash around my ankle and return the balsa board under my waist.

The sea's tenacity made itself known in fine fashion. Attempting to conquer the big drink was a fool's errand, but just as horse and human are forever allied by the saddle, so too is big blue linked to man by the surfboard. No thrashing, fighting, or curses would do me any good against the liquid mountains unless I wanted to be crushed. My power came in riding the rolling tide, harnessing the violence of nature to experience the slightest moment free from that very thing. The ocean yanked me back toward nightfall yet again. One after the other, I plunged my hands into the water below like the oars of an ancient battleship fleeing a chasing foe. Forward, forward, I pushed. Head high, chest raised, I kept on swimming until my feet were lifted overhead, sending me down the surface of the swelling element. And then I stood, first leaning heavily on my backfoot, arms flailing as if trying to fly, until I arrived level with the shore once again. Water curled above as I let myself sink deep within the surging tube. The rest is beyond words. Gods don't speak to mortals in a common tongue. The only true liberty they provide comes to those who tap the source of their providence: those who ride the creases of their divine, swatting hands.

I planted a salty kiss on my man as I returned to the sandy beach. My little girl wrapped herself around my leg and pointed toward the fading twilight. The ships grew larger since the evening session on the water. They seemed to be headed toward the island from across the vast Caribbean.

"Let's get some dinner," I said, eyes fixed toward the ships. "Mama's hungry."

Sparks from the fire burst toward the canopy of trees above as my husband roasted his red snapper catch over the flames. He bounced my girl on his lap while a few others passed honey wine between them. My arms felt like limp noodles in the warm, orange glow drying the salt across the surface of my skin. Air popped from the burning timber as if keeping some imperceptible, cosmic time with the near, audible tide. We did what human beings do best: we ate, shared stories, and drank together. Before long, we experienced another of humankind's greatest skills. The kind that brings us together for all the wrong reasons.

I awoke in our thatched-roof cabin in the sand. The honey wine filled my bladder. Leaving my sleeping man wrapped around our infant daughter, I stepped out of the shelter into the blue moonlight. Stars broke through the canopy of palms above. A cool sea breeze ran across my naked body. Crabs scuttled across the sand around my bare feet. I wrapped my hands around the trunk of a young, white oak and squatted to relieve myself. Then I heard what sounded like rumbling thunder. Not a single star was hidden behind a cloud so far as I could see. Just beyond the treeline that gave way to the beach, it sounded as though mythical giants were stomping their way ashore. The sand began to quake beneath my feet. If I hadn't already been doing so, I probably would have wet myself in fear. I stood and gazed into the deep, dark direction of the commotion. And then, as if leaning my head into the gaping throat of a dragon, a stream of fire came rushing towards me. I dropped to the sand to avoid the shooting flames, but the heat scorched my bare back. The pain didn't have a chance to set in as every cell in my nervous system turned its attention to my husband and sleeping babe. Before I could even stand to defy the onslaught of carnage, I turned to my cabin, my home, the sanctuary of all the love I knew on earth, and watched as some foreign sorcery blew the structure and my family into shards of wood, bone, blood, sand, and flesh. The explosion took me higher off the ground than the curling waves of the earlier surf. Being tossed through the air by the gods once again — weightless amidst the screams and flames — was the last thing I remember before absolute darkness consumed me. Such gloom would never again release me from its grip.

* * *

I awoke in a shallow grave of sand and ash.

The smell of burnt flesh was not foreign to me for all the hogs slaughtered and roasted on spits at village gatherings, but my mind distinguished the stinking scent of seared, human meat from the long-gone joyous feasts. Gulls and other sea birds circled in the sky. They moaned and complained about aerial views of the torched coastline. I tossed palm fronds off my chest and brushed seashells from my face. My scalded back rubbed against the coarse sand beneath me, and I wailed in excruciating pain. The sea called me to its healing waters, but as I attempted to roll over onto my front to crawl, I was distracted from my burns by my broken legs. Shooting pain stemmed up my shins from the fallen palm tree pinning me down. I shrieked yet again. Barely able to catch my breath, I took in the surrounding scene. The village was razed to the ground. The forest that once covered us was reduced to charred stumps. Smoke had overtaken the blue sky. Crackling gunfire rang out in the flaming trees that climbed the rolling hills toward the mountains further inland. The warships on shore were burning too. More gunfire amidst the crashing waves. More screams from within the caverns of my soul.

A young man in a green helmet and military uniform appeared above me. He crouched in the sand by my side. Whatever words spewed from his mouth made no sense to me. Panic and compassion were written across his face. He waved his hairy arms frantically, motioning for others to join us at my place amongst the wreckage. Together with three other strangers, the young man lifted the trunk of the fallen palm from my legs. I was dragged out of my hole and placed on a makeshift stretcher. Once again, I found myself disconnected from the earth below as they ferried me over the beach. My arms dangled over the side of the carrying bed while my eyes fell upon the beached ships I'd seen approaching from the horizon in the evening before the eradication of my existence. I must have angered the gods in my dance upon the water. They lashed out in retribution. My wrath was yet to be felt. I vowed that very moment: even the titans would fear the sound of my name.

My eyes again opened to a foreign scene.

I was surrounded by a white canvas tent. My bandaged body was one in a long row of cots. Wind shook the cloth walls as if pushing the raised sails of a ship. As my vision returned, I wiggled my extremities, sniffed the sea air, and removed the long, plastic tube extending down my throat. The harsh pain was drowned out by the countless other ailments that sent agony rushing in. I had no voice to scream. Deep breaths and tears were my only solace.

I looked at the few faces not covered in gauze staring up from the sterile, white sheets on the seemingly endless beds of injured people. A freshly shaven face topped by salty, black hair came over me. The youthful appearance belonged to the young man who rescued me from the ashes. His lips moved. My ears pricked up from their slumber.

"You were unconscious at least six days before we found you," he said. "Your eyes only opened a few moments before falling back to sleep. The coma lasted almost three months." Like all young men, he seemed to be in an inextricable hurry. "What's your name?"

A parched cough escaped my lips. I was determined to force my many questions through my aching windpipe.

"I beg your pardon, miss. What a way to wake you. Forgive me. I'll call the nurse," said the nervous young man. He turned to leave my bedside. It seemed as though he'd been there a long time. I grabbed his wrist before he could go. There was no need for a nurse. Only a soldier held the answers I required.

"Family?" The first letter caught my front teeth to my dry lips before the rest of the word fell from my sandpaper tongue.

"We combed the beach for others." He paused, no longer in such a hurry. With all my strength, I pulled him closer. My eyes were full of enough tears and rage to demand the details of my life's ruin. "You were the lone survivor of the locals, miss." He waved his arm over the sea of fallen figures without taking his eyes from mine. "You reside among the soldiers now. We'll protect you." An infirmary is no place for promises of safety. It was only my great and terrible thirst that kept me from pointing out my distrust. The soldier could see the cotton collecting around my mouth. He offered me his military-issued canteen. Water poured down my cheeks. My jaw creaked within my skull.

"Who—?" My question came forth in a breathy whisper. I held my grip on the young man's wrist as I choked on the water.

"Sergeant Antoine Porto, at your service," he responded proudly.

"Who did this to me?"

"That's a complicated question." He searched for words with a pensive stare. "You've lived here all your life?"

I nodded my head, "yes".

"You know nothing of the West Caribbean Union?"

I shook my head, "no".

"My god. There's so much to tell you, miss. You must rest. The nurse will give me hell for greeting you like this. Surely a doctor would know better—" For all my months asleep, it seemed no one had tended to my nails, so I dug them into Antoine Porto's skin. "Yes, miss. You need to know." The Sergeant cleared his throat. I could see him rummaging his mind for what to say. "Our tiny island in the middle of the Caribbean is no longer the safe haven it once was. Can you read and write, miss?"

Once again, I nodded, "yes", lying for the most part. Antoine exhaled and rubbed his forehead with his one free hand. Sweat began to bead on the tip of his nose.

"You've seen maps?"

The relief on his face was evident when I again bowed "yes" to the question. Little did he know I meant figures etched in the sand.

"OK, but still, where to begin?" He asked rhetorically. "You must forgive me, miss. This is not a simple story. I will do my best to explain, but please, I will need my hand to draw for you."

I released him from my grasp. It was clear in his eyes that he was a good man doing his best. From his breast pocket he withdrew a small notebook and pencil. Antoine went across the tent and brought a small wooden chair next to the cot. He sat close, flipping to the blank centrefold, placing the bound paper down on my bed.

"May I?" He asked.

"Yes," I managed to say, sipping the water slowly, gradually turning my mouth from parched desert to shallow puddle. The Sergeant drew vague, meandering shapes between the pages. He kept closing his eyes, making figures in the air with a pointed finger, before sketching whatever it was he tried to envision.

"This is our world laid flat." Antoine held the small book for me to see. "You have seen something like this before?"

"Countries." My tongue no longer stuck to the roof of my mouth. My throat still felt like a gravel pit.

"Yes. Exactly, miss. This is the Earth. Here is the land." Antoine shaded in the borders of the continents, leaving the water blank. I'm not sure if he thought me brain dead or stupid, but I didn't have the means to let him know I was neither. "This is where we are." Using the tip of his pencil, he pointed to a small shape hovering just above the crease between the two pages. The shaded figure resembled our village symbol for infinity. I knew the outline to be the border of my island. "Long ago, all of these pieces of land were once a single stretch of vast, dry ground. See how the outlines seem like they could fit together like a puzzle? Do you know what a puzzle is, miss?"

"Yes, damnit. Hurry, man." I was no longer at the mercy of complete silence, but I was still captive to Antoine Porto's oratory shortcomings.

"Of course. Well, you see, billions of years ago, before nations or maps ever existed, there was only Pangaea. That's the name we've given the supercontinent, the lone landmass in all the world: a great island for terrestrial life to explore. One day, the vast, single nation began to break apart. Some say the gods wanted to divide the people amongst themselves. Science says the great shift was caused by the tectonic plates moving beneath our feet like rafts on the ocean. Just below the Earth's crust are layers of minerals that form and move depending on the heat and chaos of the molten mantle just below. I was a student of science before I was a soldier."

"What does this have to do with my husband, my daughter?" It took the Sergeant a moment to realize I was speaking. The dry soil of my throat was yet to soak up enough moisture to feed the roots of my speech.

"Apologies, miss. We're getting there. I left school for the army. I'm no scientist or historian, I just want you to understand the horror that's found you. Should I continue?"

"Please."

"I'll try to move quickly," Sergeant Porto took a deep breath. "It took the gods hundreds of millions of years to tear Pangaea apart, hundreds of millions of years more to bring the rugged shapes to where you and I have seen them on a map. It's mostly oxygen, silicon, and magnesium beneath the plates. Events beyond my understanding cause these elements to flow at certain speeds. We experience these moving rafts of the Earth when they slide or collide. Earthquakes, tsunami's, volcanic eruptions, mountain peaks, and border lines are all affected by the flux of the plates. Our lives have been likewise changed because of them.

"For the billions of years it took to disband Pangaea, the leading minds on the subject believed any similar event would take millions of years to happen again. Even tiny movements of the plates can cause catastrophe. It seemed unimaginable that a hundred years would see any real change, but surprise exists to oppose expectation, I guess. Over a hundred and fifty years ago, signs of what was to come started happening. The materials beneath the crust of the Earth were churning and the plates began to converge at unthinkable speeds. Some believe the gods are ready to reunite their people upon a huge, great land once again. I don't see it that way. Pangaea is a display of wrath, not reunion." I again pressed my fingernails deep into Antoine's forearm to remind him that my questions were urgent.

"Natural disasters are rampant across the world. Nations are at war about the changing boundaries of country and responsibility. Diplomacy is as extinct as the dinosaurs that once grazed our planet. You may know it by a different name, but our island is now called the West Caribbean Union. We are among the very few countries relatively untouched by natural disaster. Now, we are among the greatest victims of human disaster. We have been invaded by our neighbours to the East. The East Caribbean Republic is sinking. They have arrived on our shores. They took the lives of your daughter and your husband. We are at war."

If I failed to leave my place in the shanty home built by my father before sunrise, I was likely to catch a few licks from the end of his stick. The schoolhouse was a little over five kilometres away. My hide would be twice as red from our teacher's ruler if I didn't arrive before morning exercises began. Tardiness wasn't an affliction I suffered often. I took my seat between my best friends.

Vallah Desear wasn't a whole year older than her brother Cash, but she was like most girls: maturing in body and mind at a pace our primary gang strived to match. Cash scratched at the wood tabletop before him with a loose nail he found somewhere in the schoolyard. Carmen was at the desk behind me. She liked to brush her lone pencil against the hairs on my neck to mimic the mosquitoes that vastly outnumbered the students in the schoolhouse. Carmen didn't have the appetite to annoy me while one of our own found himself in the clutches of our teacher's authority — which was both barbaric and enraging through our childhood eyes. Mick stood in front of the schoolhouse. He was the only one in the class taller than Vallah. Such things carried great weight at that age. We flinched with every thwack brought down on his hands. I averted my eyes to take solace in Vallah's beauty. I loved her even then. She kept her eyes on the assault taking place before the class — not reveling in the brutality but refusing to look away. A shit-eating grin was plastered on Mick's face.

His smile earned him a few extra measures of pain. As Mick's last smack was issued with fervor, our teacher's ruler snapped in half, and a thunderous crack rang out across the lands each student called home. Our teacher was distracted from doling out his punishment and wondered, as we all did, at the source of the treacherous sound.

"To your seat, Mr. Tatum," our teacher directed Mick before cautiously stepping out of the schoolhouse. Mick took his place in front of me. Furious pops and bangs increased in rhythm and volume outside. We sat nervously in our seats before our teacher returned; panic was smeared across his face, and terror was in his eyes. "Under your desks, children," he yelled over the approaching blasts and rattles before running out the schoolhouse door. We did as instructed, fearing the ruler far less than the mysterious mayhem intensifying beyond the schoolhouse.

Hours passed before we realized our teacher wasn't coming back. The wave of screams, explosions, and gunfire seemed to wash over us. My classmates grew exhausted from weeping for hours on end, and an eerie calm remained as the sun began to set. Many curled up under their desks to sleep. Even the crickets went quiet that night. I couldn't place the feeling at the time, but before I knew what the morning would bring, before I realized no one was coming for us, before I saw the hard road ahead that spelt out a childhood on the streets and a life in the ghetto, I relished the night spent sleeping next to Vallah. She slept so soundly, so closely. Her peaceful presence was my introduction to romance. Years would pass before I could name or define the comfort she gifted me by merely existing nearby. For all the fright of the day, for all the dread in the night, I cursed the sun for rising. Daybreak woke Vallah from her slumber and sprung her to action. She was the first of us to rise from beneath our desks. My heart stopped beating when she poked her head from the door into the red morning light. She waved us all over without a word. Her age limited her vocabulary to describe the carnage waiting outside the schoolhouse. A hundred years on Earth wouldn't grant a soul the words to convey it. The once lush display of nature's glory was replaced by the blackened, charred remains of villagers and soldiers. Thick, grey smoke hovered overhead, usurping the green canopy that once sheltered us from above. Such a description does the horror no justice, but what fairness does such treachery deserve in its depiction?

I recognized the smell of burnt flesh from the funeral pyres made to honour my departed grandparents. There was no trace of such a tribute for the dead spread across the ash and sand. I was not alone in my helpless need for the soothing embrace of my mother and father's arms. Each child had a different walk ahead. We were left alone in the pursuit of our families, but we didn't part ways without a plan. I thank the heavens every day for that plan. Without agreeing to return to the schoolhouse, without the promise of finding one another again, it was likely Carmen, Mick, Vallah, Cash, and I would have died before the week was out. The five of us swore to report back, to find out what brought about the end of days as we saw it. We formed our army on the spot. Even amidst my nauseating anxiety, I still managed to feel a tinge of jealousy as I watched Vallah take Cash's hand as they walked off into the thickening smoke to find their parents. All I wanted that instant was to feel her fingers interlocked with mine as I set out to discover the fate of my own mom and dad.

The usual route I used between the schoolhouse and my home was beaten by a decade of pupils travelling the path. All evidence of the trail was veiled in the scorched palms, airborne soot, and my terror. Instinct guided me along the slow, harrowing journey. With every step or burn from the embers infiltrating my sandals, I considered turning back. Monsters lurked in the black, wispy air. I swatted at the larger ashen flakes but had no desire to reveal the source of all the moans and shrieks. My eyes were scalding. Every cough clawed at my throat. And then I saw it. The home my father built was razed to the sand. The radiant, floral dress my mother sewed stitch by stitch was stained in bursts of blood. Her back was to me as her limp body lay draped across my motionless father. A dull machete lay beyond his reach from his resting place in the fine white grains where he lived out his humble life. I tried to go to them, but the flames spilling out from beneath the tin roof of my home were too hot to go any closer. A wall of heat and sorrow burnt my tiny fingertips as I reached out in helpless anguish. I was totally alone and helpless to the flames eroding my parents' faces. It was as if the son they would have raised me to be was burning away with their flesh; my blood of their blood soon whisked away in the air.

Shock engulfed me until consciousness finally returned. All I could think to do was turn on my heels and flee. My lungs went into overdrive for all my crying and reckless running. I chased any sight of thinning darkness as fast as my legs could take me. Any break in the black cloud surrounding me was a beacon. Somehow, I emerged from the treeline, from the suffocating, heavy air, and set eyes upon the schoolhouse. It was then that my legs seized up, my vision blurred, and I crashed face-first onto the earth. Vallah was the first thing I saw when I finally awoke. She was upside down, sitting over me, my head resting in her crossed legs.

"He's up," she said, as Mick, Carmen, and Cash came into view above me. There was the slightest hint of blue in the sky behind them.

"Guess he didn't find anyone either," Mick added, which I hardly understood in my haze.

Nightmare and reality converged: all my innate, infant fears about navigating the daunting world alone had come to fruition. That immediate alarm I felt from time to time when my hand fell from my mother's grip in the crowds at the market, that lingering dread I sensed when my father rowed his boat out to sea in the morning, that brief insight into the frailty of my safety and comfort materialized in my sudden mourning for my blissful childhood. Age no longer defined the chapters of my life. The genesis of my manhood was marked when Vallah embraced me to her chest to weep, it was depicted in the snot and tears my face left behind on her shirt. My manhood began when I was helped to my feet by those likewise exposed to the abrupt, crushing weight of loneliness.

"It's alright." Vallah ran her fingers down my cheek. "We won't leave you."

My descent into hell was accompanied by an angel. Her feathered wings caught fire in the fall, but her grace remained. She was a frightened seven-year-old child too. Only when looking back can I fully marvel at her nerve in the face of such doom. Vallah took us under what endured of her wings as she led the way up the coast. We walked with the wind for weeks after the raids, putting the breeze at our backs to leave the flames behind, to seek out a piece of shoreline untouched by war. As we traced the beach — scavenging for food in the charred remains of the towns and villages — only scraps were found. Our short strides were hampered by hunger and thirst. We had lived simple lives before, but quickly learned that our parents sheltered us from the fact that survival is far from simple. Our despair took brief reprieve when we happened upon a boat anchored just offshore in the distance of some other nameless village lost to the ages.

A boat presented a rare taste of hope. The five of us leapt into the sea with the closest thing to joy we'd felt since making our way to the schoolhouse that unforgettable morning, a lifetime of suffering having passed in the meantime. The cool Caribbean waters washed some of the soot from beneath my fingernails as I savoured the silence awaiting just below the surface. I opened my eyes in the crystal-clear liquid, and gazing through the salty ocean at the reef, I was reminded that life was abundant and full of colour. I was reminded that my past self was once sustained by the sea.

The vessel was made of sturdy wood, bleached under the relentless sun. It swayed gently in the calm, turquoise surf rolling toward shore. I arrived at the basic canoe first, feeling the salty water drip from my tangled hair as I grabbed the side and lifted my head above the lip. Just as I peeked over the edge, a piercing squawk sent me falling back into the cool, blue ocean.

"What is it?" Cash called out, swimming in my direction, the others close behind.

Carefully rising above the gunwale, I looked upon a massive bird flailing wildly in the bow of the boat. The shrieking monster was tangled in thin, nearly clear netting. It must have gotten itself caught while trying to make easy pickings of the fisherman's catch. I was desperate for the taste of fish too. I had that in common with the bird. The creature let out terrible sounds in its struggle as I tipped the canoe lower to throw myself over the side and into the stern. I recognized the yellow head and orange-tipped beak of the brown pelican. My father often relied on their plunging, hunting attempts to decide where to cast his nets. The same pale, blue eyes that scanned the ocean for food stared at me in sudden recognition. Two wooden paddles lay flat in the hull. My gaze fell on them. The bird took notice and began to flap wildly in its confines. As Vallah arrived at the side of the boat, I took up an oar in two hands, lifted it above my shoulders, and brought it down with all my strength on the lemon-coloured head of the bird. The pelican twitched for a moment. I clubbed it again.

Mick built a fire with mildly unsettling delight. Carmen and Vallah fashioned a small spit from driftwood. Cash cast the reclaimed net toward the sunset. I plucked the bird. Pelican is a greasy, overly fishy meal, but we dined on its meat as if it were a royal feast. The smiles I noticed in the firelight were the first I'd seen since before our teacher's cracking down on Mick's wrist all those weeks prior. We mimicked our parents and clonked our cracked open coconuts together before guzzling the refreshing water within. The canoe sat overturned in the sand nearby, promising shelter for the sleep to come.

STRICKLAND RIVER
MARCH 2192

Windshield wipers didn't do shit against the dust. The little specks just blew across my view like a cloud of gnats. I rolled up my windows. The fuel light was blinking orange in the dash of my baby. She was thirsty. There was only one small, plastic gas tank left in the back of the deep green jeep, and gas stations were few and far between in those parts.

My payload made all sorts of annoying noises as we rumbled our way across the uneven roads leading through the low hills towards the sea. Being stranded on the roadside with my catch in the back was not a scenario I would have ever wanted. I kept my foot heavy on the gas pedal.

The dust eventually settled slightly. I saw a lone pump beside the road. A man in coveralls stood next to it. His eyes were wide open as if the dirt were welcome in his gaze. Dried mud collected in the deep crevices around his eyes, cheeks, forehead, and mouth. He did not greet me with a smile. I got out my jeep.

"Fill 'er up with supreme," I said.

"Only got regular, sir," the attendant replied. His name was stitched in messy, red thread across his filthy, one-piece uniform. It read, "Carl". My catch tossed her body against the sheet-metal interior of the jeep. The vehicle swayed back and forth.

"Ain't got much of a choice then, do I?" My back was already turned to the old man as I marched toward the wood-paneled shack a few paces from the pump.

I entered the dirt-floor store. A little cashier stood silent behind the wood counter. She couldn't have been more than eight years old. Her eyes followed me as I walked along the lone, mostly empty aisle. I blew dust off the expired bags of potato chips and beef jerky I picked up. The girl seemed to flinch at the sound.

There was a bunch of bananas stacked on the counter the girl was peeking over. The fresh yellow fruit seemed to glow in the otherwise brown and hazy air. I put my two parcels on the counter and added a banana to my purchase. The cashier picked up a pad of paper and a pencil and wrote down the cost of each item. It took her a moment to tally the price.

"Four dollars and seventy-five cents, mister. You can pay for the gas outside."

I pulled my genuine leather wallet from my back pocket. The change pouch offered no coins. The centrefold held no bills. I reached for my belt, pulled out three .44 caliber bullets, and placed them down before the cashier.

"There you go," I said.

"We got no use for bullets, mister."

"Everyone's got use for bullets. It's a fair trade." The girl was visibly intimidated as I leaned over the counter. "Is that your daddy out there?" I motioned outside.

"Grandad," said the child.

"I'll go square things with him. Don't worry. You have yourself a lovely day."

I exited the store with the chips, jerky, and banana, leaving the little girl to stare at the bullets I'd paid her.

Dust managed to get behind my sunglasses as the wind kicked up on my walk across the lot. Carl was placing the hose back on the pump.

"Seventy-seven dollars. Full. Regular," he said.

"I got a spare tire in back. Lots of good rounds."

"We accept cash only, sir."

"You must be that girl's Grandaddy. She must've got her smarts from you, considering the way you both ask for money when you got no want for accepting it. Is bartering dead? I have goods of equal value to the goods I've acquired. If you got a problem with my form of payment, then that problem is yours, friend."

"I'm not your friend," Carl replied quickly. His eyes shifted to the rear compartment of the jeep.

"What kind of customer service is this? First, you don't take my respectable offer to trade, and now you're being rude. Do your job." The muffled cries of my passenger were audible through the restraint I tied to stuff her mouth.

"I have done my job."

"And how hard was it?" Sweat was beginning to collect round the brim of my hat. "You managed to fill my baby with gasoline below the standard she deserves and read out the numbers on the pump. You know what I do? You know how I make my living?"

"I can guess." He tilted his head toward the back cabin of my jeep, toward the stymied screams. Carl got a little ahead of himself, so I put my hand on my gun and leaned closer.

"Well, let's hear it," I said.

"You're a Catcher."

"That's right, old man. I'm a Catcher. The best. You want to talk to me about doing your job? I do my job for Union. I risk my neck